This is my favorite part, thirty feet above the ocean, falling at a hundred and ninety miles an hour. Close enough to see our reflections hurtling to meet us. It's the second just before the agitator lasers ahead to break the surface tension that's the sweetest. When all the adrenaline of a ten-thousand-foot free-fall culminates in a terrifying second of, "Oh, shit."

A hundred things could go wrong. The agitator may not move enough water out of the way. The air pocket could collapse before entry. The subroutine that mixes water and air for the controlled deceleration may miscalculate and flatten me into a shark pancake. Almost a hundred different ways to die in under a tenth of a second.

I love it.

Other works by Jeffrey A. Ballard

Novels:
The Oracle Algorithm

Novellas:
The Bear that Painted the Stars
The Watchers

Novelettes:
The Kerephrine Reaction
Underwater Restorations

Short Stories:
The Cancer Under St. Paul's
The Highlight of a Life
Voices in the Deep
The Skim Job: An Underwater Restorations Short Story
(July 2015)

Collections:
Vacationing Offworld:
Ballard's Speculative Collection 1

Underwater Restorations

Published 2015 by New Rochester Publishing, LLC.

First Published in *Orson Scott Card's Intergalactic Medicine Show*, Issues 37 & 38.

Cover art copyright © Robert Adrian Hillman/Dreamstime.com
Book and cover design copyright © 2015 by
New Rochester Publishing, LLC

ISBN-13 978-1-941557-20-4
ISBN-10 1941557201

UNDERWATER RESTORATIONS

by
Jeffrey A. Ballard

NEW ROCHESTER
PUSBLISHING

THIS IS MY FAVORITE PART, thirty feet above the ocean, falling at a hundred and ninety miles an hour. Close enough to see our reflections hurtling to meet us. It's the second just before the agitator lasers ahead to break the surface tension that's the sweetest. When all the adrenaline of a ten-thousand-foot free-fall culminates in a terrifying second of, "Oh, shit."

A hundred things could go wrong. The agitator may not move enough water out of the way. The air pocket could collapse before entry. The subroutine that mixes water and air for the controlled deceleration may miscalculate and flatten me into a shark pancake. Almost a hundred different ways to die in under a tenth of a second. I love it.

Then it passes and we're down fifty feet underwater and descending. Only when the static of the comm comes online through my earpiece, trying to make a connection, do I remember to breathe. The rush of the entry fades into focus on the job at hand.

Another fifty feet later, we stand on an exit ramp from I-95 and the rookie, Winn, brings up the holo-map with incomplete sonar data overlaid. Hurricane Gretchen passed through last night and did us the favor of muddying up the waters, an expected development—the Feds are just as blind.

"Lovers, you're all clear." I can hear the smirk in Puo's voice, ten thousand feet above in the *Seagull* and driving north in the South Florida Memorial Airway.

"We descended four miles too far to the east." Winn points at the blinking dot on the holo-map. "I think we'll need to jetflow. Listen, about last night—"

The flow jets will make too much noise; the squiddies are tuned to it. Its only purpose is to outrun the damn things. "No, we'll have to jump, skip, and hop to the site. It's quieter and doesn't disturb the water as much. Adjust your buoyancy in rhythm to your jumps and try to keep up." I initiate my jump subroutine and leap.

Puo. That nosy punk's always got to stir the pot. I land forty feet away at an intersection and wait. Let Winn struggle; I'll send over the subroutine after he falls several times. It's just a fling. My father always said we Schmidts think with our cocks. Well, in my case, insert the female equivalent.

Winn is still just standing there. "Rookie, what's taking you so long? Let's move."

"I'm writing a subroutine to automatically manage the buoyancy adjustments. I can transmit it to you when I'm done."

"That's very kind of you, Rookie," Puo breaks in. "Don't you think that's nice, Isa?"

"Puo—" He is so going to pay for this. "—focus on our pickup. Rookie, nice thought, here you go. I don't have time to wait for you to flounder through it." I transmit the subroutine.

Soon enough he's leaping as well. I keep one leap ahead of him as we make our way to the destination. What's left of the urban sprawl of South Florida passes by in blue-green shadows. Most of the buildings are intact, some are collapsed, but all of them are still. They seem to defy the churning of the water from the hurricane that passed through.

With less than a mile to go, alarms start going off: squiddies—the autonomous eyes and ears of the Federal Government below the waves.

I cancel the subroutine and look for a place to hide. There's a Chick-fil-A thirty feet away. I glide through a broken window and hug up against the ceiling in the play area. Hopefully, Winn's done something similar.

What are the squiddies doing this far west and north? There's nothing out here they should care about. The juiciest loot is in Miami and along the old coast. South Florida isn't even in the top ten of the most federally protected underwater sites.

I move smoothly between the top of the slide and the roof, trying not to stir any silt. The more obstacles between me and the squiddies, the better the chance their sonar can't find me, particularly after a hurricane.

A tense half hour later Puo says over the comm, "It's gone. It's two miles south and continuing to move in that direction."

"It was supposed to be clear," I say.

"They changed the modulation on the carrier frequency." His voice is agitated. "I got it now. There's definitely a swarm of them farther north than normal, but they're hanging out by the old coast. The President must be looking for some electoral year victories or somethun'."

Catching grave robbers of the sunken state is definitely a low-risk, high-profile political victory. Too bad we don't have enough credibility to tell the masses the Feds do the same thing. The real reason they police it outside of public opinion is to protect their claim.

"Rookie, check in."

"I'm here, one block over in a half-collapsed gas station. I wasn't sure whether to break comm—"

"Hurry up and meet me at the site."

***

A school of mackerel hover around an old land car, an Audi, and duck inside as I approach. Too bad Audi couldn't use that in their marketing campaign, "Over a hundred air miles to the gallon now, an artificial reef and home to thousands for Mother Earth later." It'd get the dry-earth-humpers off their backs.

The mansion looks like every other one on the block. Spanish-tile roof, arched entries, horseshoe driveway and covered in algae and buds of coral.

After eighty-six years the wood backing the eight-foot wrought-iron door is rotted and feeble. It's no match for my Kung Fu fist.

The entryway's actually kind of tasteful, notable only in the absence of the ostentatiousness of the rich trying to live like the wealthy. No statue or fountain, no pointless two-curved stairway or cheesy hand-carved table with an over-sized vase. The marble floors open to a main living area that looks out on the back through a wall of broken windows.

Not long after, Winn shows up and I lead him wordlessly upstairs and down a hallway. I carefully step over the skeleton of a canine and direct Winn to do the same. I don't know why the pets bother me so much; I barely even notice human remains anymore.

The stupid owners either left him behind or didn't listen to the warnings when the mega-quake hit in the middle of the Atlantic. It all happened sixty years before I was born, but the event has been so dissected, practically everyone is an expert on it. Long story short: huge earthquake, tsunami warnings, complete ignorance of the brand new volcanic mountain range birthed in a matter of days and continuing to grow even now. The ocean doesn't mind; it makes room where it can—goodbye thousands of miles of coastland, goodbye hundreds of major cities, goodbye entire states.

I stop in front of the last door and initiate a scan. Nothing. Still, I send Winn in first—it is a tryout after all.

"The room's secure," he says. "The sculpture's here and looks to be in decent condition."

Jug Self-portrait by Paul Gauguin, a three-quarter foot stoneware mug from the late nineteenth century. Gauguin's more known for his paintings, but there's a market for his sculptures as well.

"Puo, we're ready for pickup in ten minutes."

"Roger. There's a McDonald's Airstation a few miles ahead I'll stop at and turn around. Want anything?"

"Yeah, a large fry. Rookie, want anything?"

"Uh...no, thank you."

It's good to keep Puo on his toes. Now he'll wonder if he should get the fries and risk getting yelled at for the waste of time, or risk getting yelled at for not getting them. Either way, I get to yell at Puo.

"All right, Rookie, let's see what you got." The mug's encrusted and stuck to its resting place in eighty plus years of ocean crud—a result of the Atlantic homogenizing its new territory. When we go through official channels, the sculpture gets graded and then it's all about how damaged it is. It's critical to get it back to the shop with as little disturbance as possible. The less crud on it when we get it back to the shop, the better the equipment can restore it. A deft hand is required. A surgeon's hand preferably, hence the rookie, Winn. Sculptures don't sue for malpractice.

Winn lives up to the hype. His movements are smooth and deliberate. He gets the mug out in about half the time it would've taken me, and carefully wraps it up for transport. Impressive.

"Not bad, Rookie. Follow me to the extraction point." We get there a few minutes later—it's only fifty feet from the mansion. "Puo, we're in position."

"I'm five minutes out. Transmitting sync for pickup now."

"Why—"

"I got your damn fries! I'll be there in four minutes and thirty-seven seconds."

Suddenly, I have to pass four minutes and thirty-six seconds alone with Winn. I'm not going to tell him what a good job he's doing. I already got Puo; I don't need another inflated head on this crew.

I pretend to fiddle with my equipment. That doesn't work for long, though. The silence is stretched, turning into a large pointing arrow at the lack of conversation. I need to say something soon.

Winn beats me to it, "About last night—"

I don't want to have this conversation with Puo listening. "Are the goods secure?" Talk about work, that's easy.

"Yes."

"You got the pickup routine activated?"

"Yes."

"Okay, check your power and gravity levels. It's like nothing you've ever experienced."

"How different is it from the descent?"

"It's not, except it's falling in the opposite direction. Kind of like going in an anechoic chamber: it's only when normal is missing that you experience how weird it is."

The reverse-gravity suits aren't supposed to exist. There are only a handful, and as far as I know, they're still a top-secret project for the special forces. When the opportunity presented itself to look at the plans for one from a desperate engineer with a gambling problem, I didn't hesitate. I had to go to Paranoid Pete and put out a second loan on the *Seagull* and empty the bank account to boot, but it was worth it. The engineer left out some key components to try to convince himself he wasn't doing anything wrong—smart people always think criminals are idiots. But they weren't that hard for Puo to fill in.

"Okay, let's get to the surface for the pickup. When Puo's in position, the subroutine will automatically kick in, and whoosh, we'll free-fall toward the sky and onto the *Seagull*."

Winn doesn't say anything. His face is probably green. I'd tell him not to vomit, but there's no better teacher than experience and having to clean it up afterward.

It's still overcast when we reach the surface. The subroutine lights up a counter in the lower left of my helmet. Ten seconds to go. I take several deep breaths to prepare myself for the sudden reverse. Three seconds. "Remember to flip, so your feet are pointed toward the sky." One second.

You feel it first in the stomach, a feeling that something has gone terribly wrong. You're already two hundred feet in the air and climbing before the brain catches up and brings order to your system, reminds the body, this is what's supposed to happen.

I've done this enough times that my brain kicks in around a hundred feet. But something's different this time and it takes me another hundred feet to recognize it. It's Winn.

He's laughing.

***

"Rookie's gonna fit right in, huh?" Puo asks.

We sit in the driver's cabin of the *Seagull*, a ubiquitous air delivery vehicle we've modified for our purposes. We had tossed the back seats out to extend and close off the staging area and put in a trap door for the free-fall entries and exits. The door between the two areas is enough to stop the wind from buffeting whoever is driving when the trap door opens, but not enough to stop the smell of salt from pervading the cabin.

Winn's in the back changing out of the gravity suit. Getting out of those things is tricky, like trying to take off a wet t-shirt three times too small. "Yeah, he did all right."

"All right? The kid nailed it, wrote a jump routine on the spot, got the goods out in record—"

"What's your point, Puo?"

"Nuthin', just sayin' kid did a good job. We've needed someone else for ages. I was impressed that he handled himself so well, even the pickup, I mean—"

"Aww...how sweet, Puo and his man crush. But I got to say, I don't think Winn plays that way. Too bad, though, you two would make a sweet couple."

"After a night with you, you never know, he might play for the other team now. You never did say how he was." Puo looks at me for details he isn't going to get. "What's with you? Usually you're telling me how big the guy's—"

"Puo, pay attention to not being followed and your upcoming visit with Charlie." The satisfaction of Puo's face going lax is immeasurable—he knows he shouldn't have stirred the pot. I'd bet a small fortune his testicles just defied gravity all on their own.

***

Winn and I are in a hidden room we call the Island in the center of a six-thousand-square-foot loft in the middle of Atlanta. We're cleaning out and soaking the gravity suits, while Puo is off meeting with Charlie, our longtime fence and surrogate crew member. She gives us fair rates, mostly I think because we're both women. Puo's scared of her. He made the mistake of hitting on her once in jest and didn't know what to do when she returned interest. She's bigger than he is.

The loft is owned by our topside venture, Underwater Restorations. To the law-loving public, we restore and sell damaged art. It barely turns a profit, but the other side of our business does rather well. We even employ Ashley, a young, over-eager, master of fine arts to run the gallery in Charlotte.

She's perfect for it, way too happy to have her own gallery to ask questions.

The loft is on the top floor of an old manufacturing building on West Mariette Street. There are no windows and no advertising that we're here. All the restoration equipment and legitimate machinery is laid out around the center, with a small specialty elevator in the corner used for the delivery of pallets of restoration chemicals. Everything is designed to conceal the Island in the center. It even has a secret entrance. There's a six-foot replica of the sculpture *David* outside—guess what you have to pull to get in. I make Puo do it whenever we're together.

Winn is cleaning all the connectors with a toothbrush. It's laborious like digging a hole is: it's never exactly clear when you're done. Winn is growing restless. I can hear him shifting in his seat behind me. "Listen, Isa, about last night."

"What about it?" I continue to face away from him.

"I'm—I'm not looking for anything serious right now. With the malpractice suit and the insurance company screwing me over—"

"And you think I'm looking for something serious?"

"No, I mean, I don't know. I wasn't sure."

"'Cause I'm not." I turn around. "I thought that would've been clear when I said I had a date tonight." A pretentious gallery owner hit on me a few days ago when I was researching the competition. His chin almost faded into his neck, but the more people you know and can keep your finger on in the art community, the better.

Art snobs and criminals: those are the two types of people I'm surrounded by. Then there's Winn. I found him leaving Paranoid Pete's, the second most dangerous person

I know. A loan shark named for his paranoia of not getting paid back and taking premature, often violent, steps to make sure people pay. Only the Boss—the guy that runs and polices all the crime in Atlanta—is more brutal.

Pete has terrible rates, unreasonable time-lines, and preys on the desperate. And he was the only one willing to agree to a second loan on the *Seagull*.

At first, I was just interested in Winn's shoulder-width-to-waist ratio and why such a Laci—a law-abiding-citizen—was even at Pete's. After I learned his story and he checked out, I worked out a deal with Pete to have him join my crew.

"Look," I say, "this is an easy gig. We don't hurt anyone, actually save art that would be lost to the world, and get to free-fall—in both directions." He smiles at that. The crazy man really does like the reverse-gravity free-fall.

He nods in response. A man with a moral dilemma—strange.

Puo and I are legacies, born directly into a crew and without a citizen chip, off the official grid—ready made for crime. We accepted our lot as criminals before puberty. The only choice we had was deciding what type of criminals to be.

The monitor on the side of the room lights up and shows Puo coming back through the elevator from his meeting with Charlie. Puo's impending arrival is enough to shut down the conversation.

He comes through the door into the Island and only has eyes for Winn.

"How was—?" I start to ask.

"The meeting went swimmingly."

"Really?" Uh-oh, double-talk. Whenever the ocean or water is referenced out of context, it's code.

"You couldn't have asked for better day at the beach. Sun shinin', fresh worms—"

"Excellent." We've been in business long enough to have been through this before. But it's never pleasant. "Now that that's taken care of, this place is a sty. Clean it up, please. The rookie and I are going out for a drink."

"Is that a fat joke?"

"Yup, sweep it up, fattie." Whoops, Puo can be rather sensitive. I'll have to apologize later. The possibility that Winn's a mole has me rattled. "Rookie, escort me to the nearest bar."

"Uh ... I could stay here and help."

"Now, Winn."

***

Twenty-four hours later, Winn and I arrive back at the storage loft to find Puo waiting. He quirks an eyebrow at me when he notices Winn wearing the same clothes as yesterday, but says nothing. He doesn't even mention my missed date either. I don't know whether to be grateful or worried.

"It looks better in here," I say.

"It's clean, no bugs," he responds.

"So what happened?"

"The sculpture's hot, Charlie wouldn't take it. She gave me this." He slides over a federal stolen art sheet. "Look at the time stamp."

A chill runs through me. It's hours after we took it—hours.

Puo continues, "I went back and reprocessed the standard imagery the *Seagull* collects and look, the squiddies weren't just to the east along the old coast. They were waiting for someone to take it."

An aerial map of the underwater site shows up on the wall monitor. It's zoomed out enough to display thirty nautical miles around the mansion. Squiddies are everywhere, forming a ring around the mansion. I start laughing. "This is fantastic."

"What?" Puo asks, sharing a confused look with Winn.

"Oh, you're still in trouble for missing this Puo, but they set up a perimeter to catch the thieves. They have no idea about our free-fall entry and exit. They probably think we enter the water outside of the monitoring zone and sneak in some other way."

Puo flushes red. I'd get on him more about the squiddies, but it's better to let him stew. Sure enough, little beads of sweat start to form on his temples. Puo's a softie, wrapped in a large package. He'd never forgive himself if we got nabbed.

"Oh, wonderful," Puo says. "What about the very hot, very expensive sculpture we gotta unload? We need the funds to prepare for the Jacksonville job."

"I know, I know." Interesting, Puo doesn't trust Winn. The Jacksonville job is a pipe dream. We're not even close to the kind of resources we need to pull that off. I need time to think, to sort out our next move, and how to vet Winn further. He's been with us for over a month now and passed all the screening tests.

Winn makes a suggestion only a newly defunct Laci could think of, "Well, what are the Feds offering?"

***

"Isa," Puo says, "this is a bad idea."

"We've been over this." And we have, extensively. The next payment to Paranoid Pete is coming up and we have nothing. At best he'll repossess the *Seagull*, at worst he'll live up to his name, become paranoid, and act accordingly. Our only chance is to get some sort of proof of future funds from the Feds that we can turn into liquid cash on the secondary market.

Puo and I sit in the Island, monitoring Winn. Both of us are leaning over the table toward a speaker in the center.

Winn was the natural choice to send into the viper's nest of the Federal building, claiming information leading to the stolen art. Up until a few weeks ago he was a pure Laci, so he has all the proper documentation of an upstanding citizen, and nothing on his record except the bad luck of the malpractice suit.

Also, having him interact with the Feds will give us clues as to what side Winn's on. If Winn is a mole they may give us the cash more easily. In which case, we pay Pete and go deep.

We put his citizen chip back in and outfitted him with a one-way audio that piggybacked off it. Puo and I could listen in to everything and the Feds would just see a citizen chip acting normally, emitting information like it should.

The speaker picks up a woman's voice, "Dr. Roonse, I'm Special Agent Lowry, the lead agent assigned to the case. Let's find a quiet place to talk."

Winn exchanges pleasantries and footsteps come through on the speaker.

Puo and I immediately start searching for information on Special Agent Lowry.

"How long have you been in Atlanta?" she asks.

"I was born and raised here. I even went to medical school at Emory."

"You look like a native, you have that genteel air about you. Sorry about that malpractice business."

Winn stammers in surprise.

"It's in your file. Rotten luck, I must say. Usually, the jury's predisposed toward tall handsome men."

That cow. I know it's a ploy to soften Winn, but I start sorting through the search on Special Agent Lowry for a photo anyway.

"You can understand then," Winn says, "why I'm interested in that reward."

"Right through here."

A door opens and closes, and chairs are pulled out.

"Is this an interrogation room?" Winn asks.

Puo and I both go still.

"Technically, yes. It's really just a quiet place to talk away from interruption. Do you object to having this conversation recorded?" Winn doesn't object and she prattles off some identifying information for the recording. "So, Dr. Roonse, you have information that will lead to the recovery of the stolen sculpture *Jug Self-portrait* by Paul Gauguin?"

"Yes."

There's an awkward pause before she asks, "Can you please tell me what that information is?"

"Right, sorry." Winn clears his throat. "I rent a storage locker. I ... often have to spend the night. The malpractice suit left me with very little. Anyway, last night there was some activity in the locker next to mine. They were talking about a sculpture that was hot and in need of restoration before they could move it. I put two and two together and searched your page for stolen art and called." The best lies are the ones that toe the line of truth. Winn does have a storage locker but he's never spent the night there.

"Where's the storage locker?"

Winn taps his fingers on the table before speaking. "You'll have to forgive me, but I have reason to distrust authorities." Winn's voice increases a notch in intensity. "The people that are allegedly supposed to help you. The insurance company bailed on me on a technicality—" The scraping of a chair being pushed back comes through the speaker. "—and the chief of surgery even said there was nothing I could've done. Instead—"

"Dr. Roonse, please, calm down. You came to us claiming information."

I'm not sure how much Winn is acting and how much is real frustration.

"That reward money can turn my life around. What guarantee do I have you won't find some technicality not to pay?"

The reward isn't bad for a deteriorated Nineteenth-century piece of art. We could get a lot more if we cleaned it up and sold it through Charlie, but that isn't possible. The reward should be enough to cover our next payment.

"You don't," Agent Lowry answers. "But there's no reason we wouldn't pay. It's in our best interest to reward informants. Bad press otherwise. What do you do the other nights when you're not in the storage locker?"

"Motel. I work odd jobs for cash. When I can, I get a room to feel like a human again." Winn scoots his chair presumably closer to the table.

"Odd jobs? With your abilities? Why haven't you found something better?"

"One, I can't practice medicine anymore, and two, liquidating all my assets and selling all my stuff barely covered enough to keep me out of debtor's prison." Winn is almost shouting. "The IRS garnishes my wages so much to pay off the rest, that they're pointless."

"I see. What places have you worked?"

"Bars, restaurants, any place that needs an extra set of hands. I doubt they'd remember me."

"A pretty man like you? I find that hard to believe. But here is something I don't quite understand, Dr. Roonse. According to our financial people, you couldn't have sold everything off and covered the part of the debt you paid. Can you explain that discrepancy?" The sound of shuffling papers and then of papers being slid across a table echo through the speaker.

Oh, shit. There's no way they worked that up that fast. They were ready.

"Here's the thing, Dr. Roonse, no loan officer would cover that amount for a doctor that could no longer practice. Well, sorry. I meant no legitimate loan officer, a loan shark on the other hand..."

Winn needs to get out of there right now. They were waiting for him, they knew all about him. He needs to leave, *now*. Move, Winn, move!

"Isa!" Puo says. "Winn can't hear you, stop shouting."

I'm standing at the edge of the table with the speaker in my hands. I'm not sure when I grabbed it or what I yelled.

"I don't like where this is going," Winn says. "Am I free to leave?"

"No, you're not."

"Am I under arrest?" Smart man, thank God we prepped him.

"No. We're holding you for questioning for suspicious activity."

"I want a lawyer."

"We'll get you one. In the meantime, tell me about Ruby."

There it is. Puo and I lock eyes. It doesn't need to be said. Paranoid Pete got paranoid much sooner than we anticipated. Ruby is the cover name I use when dealing with him.

"Isa," Puo says, "we got to burn the Island and go deep."

I can't believe it. Pete broke the only rule we criminals have. We have to torch everything, cut all ties, disappear. Lose everything we've built.

And burn Winn.

If they release him, they'll tag him. He won't even know where we went. I got him into this mess. I agreed to send him in there. This will probably destroy the last of Winn's innocence, turning him into another jaded criminal. And I'm responsible.

"Isa!" Puo's already shoving discs and hard drives into the arc furnace. "C'mon, we gotta go!"

My body responds mechanically and I start loading what I can onto the *Seagull*. All I can think is, we'll have to change its name, but to what?

***

The next seventeen hours are a blur—the frantic flush of the Island, the transformation of the *Seagull*, disavowing

Underwater Restorations, scrambling to determine the extent of the betrayal. Seventeen hours in seventeen minutes, that's what it felt like.

I'm driving loops around the Airway 10 at two thirty in the morning in the newly minted *Pelican*, trying to figure a way out of this mess. Puo's in the next seat snoring. I'm not sure if he realizes how screwed we are or if it's a skill he's acquired being able to sleep anywhere at any time. I suspect it's a bit of both. I can't sleep, I know how screwed we are.

Almost in concert with Puo's are Winn's snores coming through the *Pelican's* speakers. The Feds never found the audio bug. We've been able to monitor everything. Winn hasn't said a word, not one to the Feds the entire time they've had him. Even to the lawyer he only said one sentence, "I intend not to say anything." And I'm pretty sure that was meant for me.

The only silver lining to this colossal stupidity is that I'm ninety-five percent certain Winn isn't a mole. He knew several of our contacts and none were being monitored by the Feds when Puo and I visited them to call in last favors.

Even so, the knowledge that Winn likely isn't a mole isn't particularly comforting. The only two outcomes I can see for Winn are either thirty years in prison or becoming a slave to Pete. If the Feds don't arrest Winn, Pete will get his hands on him. Winn's medical skills are too valuable. He'll go back to patching up thugs for Pete's conscripted army. Pete will never let him go.

The only outcome I can see that will turn out well for Winn, is if he is a mole. Of course if that's true, then he deserves to be gutted like a fish.

And around and around I go on the Airway 10.

Puo snorts and shakes awake. He wipes away some drool and sits up, looking groggy. "So, what's the plan?"

"Winn hasn't said anything to the Feds yet. They'll either arrest him or release him in seven hours. I'm not sure how to play it."

"I meant about Pete." Puo stretches, cracking various appendages. He sinks back into the seat and looks at me expectantly.

Oh, right. Why should I have to bail us out of this? Didn't I just prove my plans are epic failures? "I don't know, Puo. What is the plan? You got a plan?"

"No."

"'Cause I don't have a plan, Puo. So maybe you should pull your weight around here and come up with one for a change."

Puo doesn't say anything in return. I know I'm being a bitch, but I don't care. I abandoned Winn, burned everything I've built, cut myself off from the only world I know and, unless we take care of Pete first, he'll definitely have us killed so no one will know what he did. And Puo just sits there, calmly expecting some grand plan to set it all straight.

Puo says, "Pete busted the only rule, we could call—"

"No, absolutely not. That's a stupid idea and you know it." Calling the Boss from a position of weakness is a sure-fire way to end up working for him. Oh, he'll sort it all out, but remind you of that every time he wants something. It took a year last time to get his claws out of us. I'd rather take my chances with Pete, than end up working for him again. "Any other bright ideas?"

Puo mumbles something.

20

"What was that? Speak up, Puo."

"I said, you're the brains of the outfit. You always got a plan."

"Damn it, Puo. Not this time. And why the hell are you so calm?"

Puo smiles. "You always get like this before some really clever idea comes out. It's how you work. So go ahead and yell, it frees up your mind."

I nearly punch him. Puo is nothing if not loyal. I'm not entirely sure how I got to deserve that loyalty. Which gets me to thinking about loyalty and the situation with Pete. An idea starts to form.

Out of spite, I toy with the idea of not telling Puo, to discourage him from thinking he's got me figured out. But we have a small window before Pete finds out what happened.

"Pete's men only serve him," I say, "because they're either indebted to him, or because he provides steady pay."

"Right." Puo mulls this over. "So, we steal his stash and his men turn on him. I like it. Simple, plays to our strengths, lets others do the dirty work. So, what's the game?"

"We don't have time for a game."

"All right, old-fashioned, straightforward thievery it is. Classic. Where's the stash?"

"I don't know, Puo. Up your ass?" I'm still frustrated with him.

"Is that what that is?" Puo leans over and farts repeatedly in rapid succession. He settles back into his seat, smiling, his eyes half closed. "Mmmm...the stash is...lumpy."

Despite myself, I'm laughing. Ever since we were nine, Puo has been able to make me laugh. I vent the cabin.

"Fine," I say. "Here's my plan. Pete keeps his records in a tan ledger that he loves to lord over people. After several years in business, he's filled up quite a few of them. We need a recent one that he isn't using anymore. That'll tell us where his stash is, and since he isn't using it, he won't notice it missing."

"Right."

"He keeps them in a waist-high safe in the corner of his office."

"What kind of safe?" Safe cracking is Puo's gig. I've never had the patience for it.

"Don't know. A green one? There were five audible clicks when he opened it during one of my visits."

Puo rolls his eyes. "Isa, that's useless."

"Yeah, you're going to have come with me."

"How we gonna get in?"

Pete's office is on the top floor of a three-story building. Pete controls the area, which leaves coming in from above the only option. I smile at Puo.

"No, no way!" Puo shifts away from me as far as he can get. "I'm not wearing one of those stupid vomiting suits again."

I laugh, then mime puke exploding inside of a helmet and down my face.

"Isa, no." Puo's not above whining to get his way, but before he starts his face breaks into relief. "Besides all my tools are here, and since we don't know what kind of safe it is, I don't know what to bring."

"What? So, you want me to bring you the whole damn safe?"

Puo looks thoughtful for a second and says, "Yep, that's exactly what you should do."

***

This is not my favorite part. I love the free-fall descent, and tolerate the unnatural ascent. But bouncing between the two for the purposes of hovering—not so much. It's not even hovering, it's jerking me up and down, mixing the contents of my stomach up like some Rube Goldberg blender.

We designed the suits to work in the ocean. The extra force from buoyancy helps smooth out the motion. Buoyancy is negligible in air—it makes for a bumpy ride. There wasn't time to see if we could modify the subroutine. Even worse, the reverse-gravity modules work on a closed system, which means I'm in the full gravity suit, helmet included, jammed over my night vision goggles. My peripheral vision's cut off and what I can see is distorted through a curved glass plate. Plus, everything I hear sounds distant. I'm going in almost deaf with tunnel vision. Maybe I should've shoved nose plugs up my nose to match the motif.

I oscillate outside a window that's been filled in with brick to match the rest of the side of the three-story building. Pete's office is on the other side. I have no idea if he's in there. For this to work, Pete can't have any clue something is amiss and that means setting the laser cutter on the narrowest setting. So narrow, that I can't even fit a scope-wire through to see if the office is occupied.

I have to time the laser cutter with my mini-ascents, as I cut through the mortar. Thankfully, the brick in the window was added later so all the edges around the window are straight. There's a slight dip in the cut along the left edge, where I realized this would've been a perfect task for Winn's steady surgeon hands.

I put the laser cutter in my pack and take out handles, which I attach to the center of the brick window. I push the brick forward into the office. It slides smoothly but not easily. Two hundred pounds of brick isn't trivial to move. The moment of truth is when the brick is halfway into the office. I need to push the brick in, get into the office and reverse the gravity enough not to slam the brick on the floor. If Pete's in there, I'm a sitting duck. If I drop it, without the additional weight I'll hit the ceiling.

The gravity subroutine will help with lowering the two-hundred pound block, but I still have to hold it, it's still two hundred pounds. Holding a cannon ball descending or ascending is still holding a cannon ball. I check my gravity subroutine and get ready to push.

I pause to see if I can detect any clue about what's on the other side. I can't.

I push the block the rest of the way.

Several things happen. My arms are seriously considering life without my body. It's dark and I feel more than see that I'm descending too fast. I try to get my legs down toward the floor, but it's all I can do to keep ahold of the damn block of bricks. My legs end up parallel to the floor behind me, with the block of bricks leading the charge.

Thunk.

Even through my helmet I can tell that was a hell of a lot louder than I intended. Books, it landed on books. They softened the blow, but there's no time to waste.

I quickly search the room. No one's in the office. The night vision goggles paint the room green. The brick cutout rests squarely on several piles of books, it didn't even knock any over. The brick walls are bare, but several bookcases are set along the walls and full with either books or knick-knacks—probably trophies of some kind. Directly across from the door is an oversized desk illuminated by the light from under the door. It's a monstrous wooden thing. I wouldn't be surprised if Pete had it raised just so he could look down at people when doing business.

I turn off the gravity subroutine and take off my helmet so I can hear properly. Hopefully, if I have to bolt, I'll have enough warning to get it back on and escape.

The safe is waist high and almost as wide and deep, and at least five hundred pounds of the latest and greatest steel alloy. There's no way I'm moving this thing by hand. Which is where Puo's idea comes in.

I take Puo's modified extra gravity suit, which is the largest we have, out of my pack and start sliding it over the safe. Once most of it's stretched into position I turn it on. Even though the suit isn't a closed system yet, it's enough to generate a weak gravity field, reducing the weight enough for me to get the rest of the suit around the bottom. I seal the gravity suit and activate the hover subroutine. It rises and bounces between my chin and chest.

I'm silent for this job so I signal Puo it's ready.

Puo speaks through my earpiece, "I'm one minute and forty seconds away."

I signal back 'acknowledged.' Puo is up in the *Pelican* driving a loop in the airways around the area. Each loop takes about four minutes. Which means there's only a twenty second window every four minutes when the safe can be delivered, or I can be picked up.

I guide the safe toward the window. When Puo gives the signal—

Voices. Someone's approaching the door.

One, maybe two. I can't tell. I scoop up my helmet. The safe is blocking the only way out. I position myself to chuck the safe at the door and start to squeeze my helmet on.

The handle twists and the door shunts inward. It's locked!

I freeze with my helmet halfway on and listen over my beating heart.

"Do you have a key?" a man with a deep voice asks.

"No," another man answers, "it's Pete's office. He don't give no one keys to his office."

Oh, thank God for Pete's paranoia. That stupid bastard just bought me time.

The first man says, "Then we have to call Pete."

"I ain't callin' Pete."

"You said you heard something."

"I did."

Puo thunders in my earpiece, "Forty seconds away." I know the men can't hear Puo, but his voice is jarring. "Launch the package in thirty. Sync in three-two-one, sync."

I activate a hack of the pickup routine on the safe and push it outside the window. When Puo's in position the safe will fall into the sky.

"Fine, I'll call him," the first man says. "But you're going to tell him what you heard."

"If you're calling him, why don't you tell him? I don't want to wake Pete up."

The voices fade down the hallway the way they came. I look out the window, the safe's gone.

Fifteen seconds later Puo comes on the line again, "Package delivered, unwrapping it now."

I type the situation out on the communicator. We have probably less than ten minutes, including getting that brick back in place.

Puo's responds, "Understood."

It's all business for him now. He's in his element with the safe. Safe cracking is about as intimate as I've ever seen Puo get. I've even heard him refer to it as caressing the tumbler.

I'm tempted to go through Pete's stuff while I wait, wipe boogers on the coffee mug, run his pencils through my ass crack, that sort of junior high stuff that's stupid but so oddly satisfying. But he can't know we were here. Even though he's probably on his way right now.

If Pete catches on, this whole thing is blown. Pete needs to find something. Something that could explain the noise, justify him getting called, but stop him from looking further.

There's a bookcase with adjustable shelves by the window and the top shelf is even overloaded. I remove all the items and scatter them about like they fell. The bookcase is close enough to where I set the brick cutout down that it could justify kicking over the books when I leave to cover any debris. The laser cutter takes care of the front left-side adjustable piece that holds the shelf. A slight cut is enough for me to break the rest of it with my hands, giving it a sheared, tried-to-hold-too-much-weight look. Perfect.

It's been three and half minutes since the safe left. Pete could be here any second. I query Puo on his status and wait for a response.

And wait. And wait.

JEFFREY A. BALLARD

Four minutes and forty-five seconds. I have to get the safe back in and restore the brick wall. I resist the urge to keep pinging Puo, he's probably in the middle of climaxing.

Five minutes, fifty-one seconds. Puo speaks through my earpiece, "Got it. Repackaging and ready to drop in two minutes ten seconds."

My impatience flares. Two minutes of dead time. Two minutes for simple repositioning. Two minutes of Pete drawing closer.

Time hasn't been kind to me lately. The past eighteen or so hours have passed like minutes, now the minutes pass like hours. Every creak of the building, every noise coming from the street through the window sounds like a gunshot. It's wearing on my nerves.

And the damn musky smell of Pete's office isn't helping. I should've worn nose plugs. The smell is overpowering, almost like Pete's in the room. I can't decide if Pete uses a cologne that makes this room stink, or if this room makes Pete stink.

Finally, Puo says, "Twenty seconds out."

I force my helmet back on.

Puo continues, "Sync in three-two-one, sync."

I sync my gravity subroutine and go outside the window to direct the safe back in. The safe is falling toward me. This is a precision drop like nothing we've done before. At least when I drop, on the way down I can adjust to some degree where I'll land. The safe doesn't have arms and legs to steer. But objects don't just fall straight down when pushed off a moving vehicle. They capture some of the momentum. It's all part of the calculation and fervent prayer.

Fortunately, in a night sky that is clouded with moving objects, the safe is hard to distinguish against the background. Unfortunately, it looks like it's going to hit the edge of the roof.

Clang!

The safe clips it and spins on the way down. I'm able to corral it, but the noise is on the level of throwing a metal trash can to the ground.

Well, if they didn't hear the first noise, they certainly heard that. I get the safe back into the room, set it in place, and remove the gravity suit. I look the safe over. No scuff marks that I can see; must have hit on the bottom or back, which is fine with me.

Puo says, "Isa, a vehicle just descended and pulled in front."

Thirty, forty-five seconds at best before Pete gets here. I'm already moving.

All I need to do is move that two-hundred pound block of bricks that nearly ripped my arms off once before. I dart into my pack to get the handles and stop when I brush up against the extra gravity suit. It worked with the safe.

I put the modified gravity suit on the back the bricks first, then attach the handles.

Shadows start jumping underneath the crack of the door. They're coming.

I activate the gravity subroutine. Two-hundred plus pounds of brick magically turns manageable. I kick over the books.

I'm in the air with my ass outside the window, about to fit the bricks back in place, when the shadows stop moving again.

They're outside the door.

I might make it, they might not notice the wall right away. I line up the edges.

The left edge won't fit. The brick wall is upside down.

I freeze. It's over.

I get ready to use the blocks as a weapon. I strain and can barely hear someone's soft garbled voice. They keep talking. They're just standing there.

I seize the opportunity and flip the block around. Sweat drips down the back of my neck from the effort. They still haven't opened the door. I fit the block into place and pull it flush. I made it.

I take the handles off and remove the modified gravity suit. My adrenaline's so high I think I can hear them through the brick. I'm left with an uneasy feeling. What did I forget?

The distant voices are getting louder. They're not in the office. They're on the roof, heading straight toward me.

I use the building to leapfrog myself toward the back of the building. Silence is secondary to speed. I just turn the corner when my heart stops.

A muffled yell, followed by a back-and-forth I can't distinguish.

My eyes are glued to the roofline.

One one-thousand—two one-thousand—three one-thousand. No movement.

The muffled talking continues. They must've found where the safe hit the roof. With any luck, they'll assume it was some type of throwaway from the sky.

My body can't take much more adrenaline. I use the gravity suit to drop to the ground and make a run for it. I need to find someplace to hole up in and have Puo come pick me up. I think I might finally be able to sleep after this.

***

Three hours later I'm back on the *Pelican* getting cleaned up. What I really need is a decent shower, but I'm making do with a wash cloth and a fresh change of clothes.

After escaping from Pete's place, Puo and I decided he couldn't just drop down and get me after all. Personal air vehicles aren't very common descending down into Pete's slum. The *Pelican* would be noticed—and reported.

I ended up having to wait for public transportation to start back up and take me to a better part of town for the pickup. I passed three of the dullest hours known to man, sitting in an all-night diner in my own filth, keeping an eye on the door. I hadn't planned on taking off my gravity suit, so I sat in the diner in a tank top and black yoga pants, plastered in sweat. Fortunately, with my odor, I fit right in at the place.

Those three hours weren't completely wasted, though. Puo's been deciphering the ledger. I finish cleaning up and walk into the cabin.

Puo looks solemn, resigned.

"Well?" I ask.

"Pete stacks."

I slump into the chair next to him. Stacking is when a mark splits his stash among multiple locations. "How many?"

"Definitely four, possibly five. There's something else, Isa. Pete keeps his wealth in the physical. Jewels, precious metals and the like. Even if we could hit all the stacks, we can't physically move everything by ourselves. The *Pelican*'s too small. We can't expose ourselves to get help."

"We don't have to steal it, just destroy it or stop him from getting access."

"Isa, Pete's loaded. We could hit all but one and he'd survive."

Where's Puo's optimism now? His we-can-do-anything attitude? Suddenly, it gets hard and he wants to roll over?

"Isa, you gotta call him."

"Stop using my name, Puo. It's annoying, Puo. I'm not a child, Puo."

Puo taps the tan ledger. "Pete's embezzling."

Interesting. The Boss gets a cut of all the crime that goes down in the city. If Pete's embezzling and we have proof, then we're not coming to him in a position of weakness. We're whistle blowers doing the Boss a favor, still looked down on like scum, but maybe after everything is cleared up we could leak the true story.

But God, I hate calling the Boss. I'll be perceived as a scared little girl, "Daddy, there's a big bad man after me. Daddy, I need you to protect me. Daddy, I'm too weak to help myself." It's enough to make me sick. Pete deserves it though.

"You gotta call him," Puo repeats.

"Fine." My brain's shot. I can't think of anything else that might work. I'll make the call later at a more civilized hour.

I lean into the reclined seat. I haven't slept in almost twenty-six hours. My nerves are fried, my brain's dead, my body's exhausted. Falling asleep isn't the problem—staying asleep is.

The twenty-minute chunks are the high performers. The rest average between ten and fifteen minutes. Every time I slide into sleep, Winn is there to meet me.

His clean-shaven face gains a gray, scraggly beard. His well-fitting clothes morph into a disheveled prison uniform. The worst are the images of his hands. His soft, surgeon's hands. Steady and strong; turning into cracked, nicotine-stained skeletons bound by handcuffs.

After about an hour and half of this, I give up. Winn will haunt me waking or sleeping. At least while awake, I can block some of it out.

It's 8:00 a.m. Winn is due to be released in an hour and a half. If the Feds do release him. They're probably working overtime to pin the theft on him. Even if he is released, Pete will pick him up at the first opportunity to work off his debt.

Winn doesn't realize that he's already too deep in our world. The criminal underworld leaves a trace on a person. People who have fallen into crime hold themselves a certain way. They know where to look, linger a second too long on a cop. In Winn, this is an oxymoron. If I saw him for the first time, my thoughts would be that he's trusting, a rube, but from the trace, in trouble, panicked.

In other words, easy prey. An ideal mark, a perfect patsy. Winn will spend the rest of his life wasting away in a cell or in the hands of someone like Pete, being used and manipulated.

I can't leave Winn to this fate.

"Puo, I'm going back for him."

***

I stand in a storage closet full of restoration chemicals in the loft where the Island used to be. Owned and run by Ashley's Restorations. It wasn't even a half hour after we had turned control over to the twit that she had changed the name.

The Feds released Winn an hour ago. I had picked up a disposable communicator, and sent a one-word message to him: Island, then tossed it in the trash. The Feds will have hacked his communicator at a minimum and are going to be watching him, but we need to get Winn now before Pete gets his hands on him.

I've been waiting for twenty minutes, drifting in and out of alertness. Even after I had called the Boss, I still couldn't find rest, stuck in the same track of questions. Will he come? How angry will he be? What will I say? Will he believe me? And more importantly, will he have a visual cortex bug?

The last question bothers me the most. There's little I can do if he does, other than coldcock him and run. We don't have the equipment to deal with it anymore, and even if we could take him somewhere to deal with it, the Feds would know where and who, as well as get an image of me.

I hate waiting.

Puo speaks through my earpiece, "He's here, and he's got a tail." Puo's high in the sky in the *Pelican*, running command.

I ready my equipment and step flush to the side of the door.

Several minutes later, Winn enters, turns on the light, and walks past me. I put the end of a short metal tube I found in the closet between his shoulder blades. "Shhh."

He freezes.

I start scanning with my other hand. Sure enough, the scan picks up a tracking and audio bug almost immediately on his citizen chip. Well, good tricks are good tricks for all sides. That's one bug. I keep scanning.

Puo says, "More plain-clothed cops are showing up."

Not a good sign.

Winn starts to tense, he still doesn't know it's me. He's going to do something stupid. I lean forward and kiss the back of his neck, then nibble on his ear for good measure. He relaxes and I drop the metal tube.

I initiate the visual cortex scan. The scan itself takes only a few seconds, but then the software needs time to chug through the data before giving the results. Puo explained why it takes so long to me once. Something about how the brain communicates with tiny electrical signals that can mask the signature of the bug.

Seventy percent done. I take a deep breath. If this comes up negative, then all I have to do his remove his citizen chip and we can get out of here.

Puo interrupts the silence, "They're forming a perimeter around the building. I also think they got an unmarked air vehicle up here."

Great. I was hoping they'd be content to watch. The earlier text probably got them hot-to-trot.

Eighty-five percent done.

Puo says, "They're entering the building. You gotta get out of there."

Shit. I need to get the audio chip out before we can bolt, but the scan isn't done.

If the Feds get my image, at best my ability to work will evaporate, at worst I'll rot in a ten-by-ten concrete jail cell for twenty-three hours a day for the rest of my life. I'd be a maximum security risk—an accomplished thief, con woman, and escape artist. There probably wouldn't even be a window. For twenty-three hours a day, for the next sixty years, I'd just sit there. I'd be insane in less than a year.

Ninety-four percent done.

Puo says, "They've got dogs."

I step around front to face Winn and put my fingers to my lips to keep him quiet. I had made my choice when I decided to come here. Thankfully, he listens. He still trusts me. I expect to see anger. Instead I see fear, desperate need—that I'm his last hope. Why does he still trust me after I nearly hung him out to dry? He's like a lost puppy that deserves better.

I put the extraction device over his left hand to remove the citizen chip. Once the device indicates it's found the chip and got a lock on it, I rip the device off bringing blood and the chip with it. There isn't time to be gentle.

Ninety-eight percent done.

I set the chip in the center of the floor. I motion to Winn to add his communicator next to the chip. I open the door to the loft and wait. Attenuated dog barks travel up and out the stairwell from the first floor. Winn looks at me in alarm. His round blue eyes contrast against the straight line of his jaw. I wink back.

A hundred percent. No cortex bug.

I grab Winn's shirt and run for the corner of the loft with the small specialty elevator and climb in.

The shaft is lined with regularly-spaced bars to make the descent easy. I added them when we got the loft, as a quick escape route. I still can't believe we had to burn this place. It was perfect.

The cops are working their way up the building. As we descend we can hear cops talking to one another, giving orders. They still haven't searched the elevator. That'll probably change when the dogs get to the loft.

We reach the basement and I check: no cops. We climb out, remove a sewer grate and drop down into the sewer, replacing the grate behind us. In a couple of blocks we'll get out and Puo will pick us up.

We jog to the first turn, then slow to a brisk walk.

"You can talk now," I say.

"What happened?"

"Pete rolled on us. He figured we wouldn't find out. It was a hedge, either he'd get paid reward money if they arrested us, or we'd be successful and we'd pay him. Either way, he gets paid. He never thought we'd be so stupid as to try what we did."

"They think I'm a criminal. They wanted to arrest me."

You are a criminal. What did you expect? But I don't say these thoughts out loud. I've lived this moment; I know those words won't be helpful. It's the moment when you realize that's it, there's no going back. Mine was when I was seven. I botched picking a tourist's pocket and had to run for my life.

"I want out." His voice is small.

There is no out. The only way out is to purchase it with more money than we've ever had, which means pulling more jobs. I don't have the heart to tell him, so I say, "Okay."

He chews on his lip. "So, what now?"

"First, we need to deal with Pete. He'll know soon, if not already, that we know he ratted. He'll move against us."

Winn pales. "How'd Pete even know I was with you? All I ever told him was that I had another source of income."

"I bartered for your debt. Pete didn't let you go easily. He had his very own personal doctor to patch up his thugs, your services were more valuable than the coin. The only way I could convince him was to add your debt to mine."

"But I was still paying him. I used the money you paid me with. You took on double my debt?"

"Yeah."

He pauses, then says, "Thank you."

I can't remember the last time someone has sincerely thanked me for anything. Ashley doesn't count, she has no idea what she agreed to. "Uh, you're welcome."

"He would have never let me go, would he? Even after I worked it off?"

"Not likely."

"So how do we deal with Pete?"

"We settle the score."

***

Puo closes the tan ledger when Winn and I enter the cockpit of the *Pelican*. "Welcome back, Rookie." Puo smiles in greeting. The smile is genuine but distant. Not saying anything to the Feds for twenty-four hours does wonders for trust, but we're not completely there yet.

Winn nods his greeting and sits down. I stand behind him.

"Any progress?" I ask Puo. Time to put on a show for Winn. Hopefully, this will get us to a hundred percent trust.

"Five as far as I can tell. Two we can easily hit—his restaurant The South Grill and a small local bank. That may be enough with a fire run."

"Yeah," I say, "but with a fire run the mark is clued in."

"But it works, or we get lucky and he tries to move it, bringing it out into the open." Puo hands me the ledger, which I slip into my bag.

"Guys," Winn says, "what are you talking about?"

Hook, line and sinker. Winn really would've made a good patsy.

I answer, "Pete divides his wealth among multiple locations. It protects him against unforeseen loss, like theft. If he loses one stash, it's only a percentage of the total. We know of two locations but not the rest. A fire run is when you clue the mark in by going after the pieces you know about in a very set fashion, say every three days. In this case, the restaurant and the bank, after those are gone, the mark will assume we know the rest and will either check on them or have them moved. Either way, we're watching and will learn the location of the remaining pieces."

"And that will get him off our backs?" Winn asks.

"His men will turn on him," I say. "Half only work for him because they're indebted, the other half because he pays regularly. Take away his capital, his ability to pay, and we cut him off from his men." I sit down. "We'll hit the restaurant first."

I hope this is the last time I have to lie to Winn.

***

The following afternoon, I sit in Pete's office, waiting for the pompous ass to stop reading his *Zen and the Art of Leadership* book. I can't help but think of Winn, sitting in The South Grill restaurant at this very moment waiting for a cue that will never come.

Pete thinks it's a power play to make people wait. I should have sent Puo and loaded him up with beans. I start laughing at the thought. That gets Pete's attention.

"Something funny?"

"Just something Puo does." Normally, I'd draw this out, savor the moment, but Winn's waiting. "We couldn't unload the sculpture. Someone tipped off the Feds."

"That's not really my problem, now is it?"

"It is, since you're the one that tipped them off."

Pete leans back and subtly moves his hand along the chair's arm. To an untrained eye, it would look like he was getting comfortable. To the trained eye, he had just called for help. "That's quite an accusation. Can you prove it?"

"Nope. Very hard to go to the Feds and ask who tipped them off. One might be able to trace the money, but you didn't get paid, did you, Petey?"

The muscles twitch on one side of his face. Petey...I'll have to remember that.

Two of his thugs come to stand behind the desk on either side of him. "So you come in here with accusations you can't prove and no money. Jerome, Boots—"

"Hold on, I do have something of interest." I pull out the tan ledger and hand it to him.

I've been schooled for over twenty years, in cons, games, swindles, flimflams, you name it. Composure is the single greatest factor that affects the outcome of any of them. But I can't help but smile at his shaking hands.

He compares the ledger I handed him to the current one on his desk, then glances over at the safe. "How?" Pete starts, then collects himself. "I just checked hours ago. You haven't stolen anything."

"Nope, not a thing. Why go through all that effort when the Boss offers a ten percent finder's fee on assets people hide from him?"

It's the knockout punch. He blanches and drops the ledger. He skips over the first stage of grief and goes immediately to anger. "Jerome, Boots, kill her. Make her suffer. I don't care what you do."

Jerome and Boots shift their stance to box Pete in.

"Looks like Jerome and Boots have a new employer," I say. When the Boss learned of the situation, the first thing he did was forgive debts and offer three times what Pete paid to control his men. Much easier to have allies than a war.

The elation of victory is short lived. Pete starts to tremble. Soon I start to see that same need in Pete's eyes that I saw in Winn's. There's a reason I went into thievery and not other criminal enterprises. The look on Pete's face is it. I can't stand it. It robs the triumph right out of the moment. I wouldn't have the heart to follow through. That's why I rob underwater graves—doesn't hurt anyone.

I get up and pause halfway to the door. Pete's whimper of "please" will haunt me for years.

***

"How'd it go with Pete?" Puo asks.

"He crumbled much faster than I thought." I'm back on the *Pelican*, heading toward The South Grill.

Silence settles over the cockpit. Puo has no stomach for that stuff either.

After several minutes of fighting traffic on the Air 20, he says, "You know, with the ten percent finder's fee, we could actually pay for one of us to go legit. Pete was one rich son-of-a-bitch."

"I know." We both know we're not talking about ourselves and there's nothing left to say. The rest of the ride is in a comfortable silence.

The South Grill is a dive, a total hole—plain wooden booths, laminate table tops. There are even grease stains running all along the top of the walls. Winn is sitting in the only occupied booth, eating a stack of pancakes. I slide in next to him and Puo plops down on the other side of the table.

He doesn't say anything at first, but sips his coffee. "There never were conch shells on the beach, were there?"

Damn, the man learns quick. "No, there weren't."

He nods. "What's the point of gathering them then?"

Right to the heart of the matter. "Pete's been dealt with—definitively. You were the one to suggest going to the Feds. We needed to make sure you were clean."

He starts to object, but I interrupt him, "There was a chance Pete was playing you, even without your knowledge. We had to make sure."

"Are you sure now?"

"Yeah," I say. And we are. The restaurant's been monitored since about eight hours after we learned of Pete's betrayal. There's been no out of the ordinary activity telling us Pete had been tipped off.

The waitress comes over and I order a bowl of oatmeal with no intention of eating it and a glass of water. Puo loads up on an omelet.

"How'd you deal with Pete?" Winn asks.

"We stole his ledger," I say, "to find out where he hid his cash."

"Ahem," Puo says.

"Oh, all right. Puo, in an astounding display of skill, cracked the safe in amazingly, stupefying, mystifying speed—without which, we would have surely failed and been roasted alive. Satisfied?"

Puo bows his head.

"Anyway, turns out Pete's been lying to the Boss for years about what he made. It was easier to notify the Boss and let him do the dirty work. He'll give us a ten percent cut of what he recovers."

"I didn't realize you knew the Boss."

"He's her father," Puo says. He's calm about it, matter-of-fact about dropping one of my deepest secrets. I've sought for so long to distance myself from him. Puo remains silent and eyes me, inviting me to challenge him. I decline.

Eventually Puo caves to the intervening silence and says, "C'mon Isa, if he's gonna be a fully vested member, he's gotta know."

"Fully vested member?" Winn asks.

"The rookie's graduatin'!" Puo grins and pretends to wipe away a tear. "I'm so proud."

"You have two options," I say. "One, you stay on and help us rebuild. We could use the help."

"Is that the only reason you want me to stay on?" Winn asks. His full, honest face regards me over his pancakes. I divert my eyes to stay focused.

"Two, you go legit. Our take from the finder's fee is enough to cover the cost. You'll have to move overseas, but it's a chance at a normal life. So there it is, a way out. They don't come often." Never actually, this is the first time we've ever had the capital to try to do it.

"What about you guys?"

"What about us?" I ask. "We are what we are. It's a little hot here for us right now, so we're setting up shop in a new city." It's stressful, starting all over again.

We fall into silence as the waitress brings our food. Puo dives right into his omelet, while I ignore the gray stuff in front of me that's supposed to pass for oatmeal. The clinking of Puo's fork is the only sound at the table for several minutes, punctuated occasionally as Winn pokes at his pancakes.

Finally the silence is too much and I say, "Look, you don't have to decide now—"

I never see Winn move. One second he's next to me pushing food around on his plate and the next we're locked in a full-on kiss.

He breaks away and says, "I'm in. You're a real piece of work Isa Schimdt."

"Wait till you meet Dad," Puo says.

I'd tell Puo to shut up, but I can't. I'm not done with Winn. The maple syrup on his lips is delicious.

*The fun continues for Isa and
the gang in July 2015!*

Read on for a sneak peek.

Author's Note

Word-of-mouth and reviews are vital for any author to succeed. If you enjoyed reading this story, please consider leaving a review wherever you purchased it. Taking a moment to leave a few lines sharing your thoughts would be helpful for other readers and very much appreciated. Thank you for reading!

Jeffrey A. Ballard currently releases a new story every other month. If you want to be the first to know when a new story becomes available (and receive a free exclusive story available only to newsletter subscribers and occasional other goodies) you can sign up for his mailing list at: http://www. jaballard.com. Your email address will never be shared and you can unsubscribe at any time.

About the Author

Jeffrey A. Ballard writes and lives in the Texas Hill Country just outside of Austin. From a small child he has always been fascinated with the ocean, leading him to earn a B.S. in Ocean Engineering from FAU and a M.S. in Acoustics from Penn State.

His overactive imagination followed him into academia, where he is currently a researcher at the University of Texas. Eventually, he circled back to a boyhood ambition of writing down all his dreams/daydreams/fantasies, an active playground for that overactive imagination. He writes daily now and has found a wonderful second life for his college textbooks.

Learn more about Jeffrey at jaballard.com.

Announcing Ballard's Speculative Fiction Collection 1!

The first five stories published by Jeffrey A. Ballard are collected here into one volume including three never before published stories: the steampunkish "The Medicine Doctor," the eerie "The Chime-Hour Born," and the humorous "Human Plopping." Fun bonus material includes an introduction to every story with behind the scenes info—the story behind the story.

Available Now!

A sneak peek of:

THE SKIM JOB

AN UNDERWATER RESTORATIONS SHORT STORY

by
Jeffrey A. Ballard

Coming July 2015!

NEW ROCHESTER
PUSBLISHING

THIS IS NOT nearly as fun as my normal ten-thousand-foot free-fall entry, slinking in underwater at nighttime from the opposite shore about a mile back.

I'm forty feet down in a black plain scuba suit in Keuka Lake, the "Y" shaped Finger Lake in upstate New York, following the Cleaner's, Ham's, flabby ass. Squishy is not an adjective I generally look for in a man's ass—not that I'm interested—but the job necessitated a Cleaner and there's nothing else to look at in the dark, murky water by the low glow of our guide light, so here I am.

It's *cold* down here, much colder than I'm used to. Every time I move a limb down here, I feel an influx of chilly water penetrating into my wet suit, invading my nice body-heated warm pocket of water. Besides being colder, the fresh lake water just feels different to me than the ocean water I'm used to. It's thinner, dirtier. Slides right off, where the salt from the ocean always felt heavy, seemed to linger.

It's louder down here too, much louder, even at night. The constant whir of motor boats overhead, the increasingly repetitious crack of the Fourth of July fireworks, the parties with alcohol-degraded voice modulations.

It's the *perfect* time to hit a smart home. All the abnormal-normal distractions will jack up its false alarm rate and result in a slight desensitizing. Which is why we're underwater, eighty feet off of the shore of Waylon Lo's private lake-house, just outside the house's monitoring zone and Ham is carefully tinkering with an underwater cable. Underwater sensors are always the weakest part of a smart house security net, especially when there's a lot of lake activity.

Another firework cracks overhead, and the dark murky water around me lightens briefly. Those cracks and lightenings are getting closer together, building toward the finale. We don't have much time.

I fiddle with the fanny-pack tugging at my waist, positively buoyant from the individually wrapped water-tight bags holding goodies for the job ahead. "How's it coming?" I ask Ham's flabby ass.

"Patience is a virtue, my dear," he says, his voice oily even over the underwater comms. "Practice being virtuous."

Here's where if he were Winn, I'd squeeze his ass in response, or if he were Puo, I'd lick my finger and stick it in his ear. But Ham isn't one of my normal crew, so I resist my smart-ass nature and settle on humming *The Battle Hymn of the Republic*, a classic even two hundred and fifty years after its inception—all the fireworks have me feeling patriotic.

"Quiet," Ham commands.

Commands. No one commands me, least of all this oily prick. I start singing, "Mine eyes have seen the glory of the coming of the Lord—"

"Shut up!"

"He is tramping out the vintage where the grapes of wrath are stored—"

"Will you shut up!"

"He hath loosed the fateful lightning of His terrible swift sword: His truth is marchinggg onnn!" The fireworks cracking overhead strengthen the rejoinder.

"You hired me for me this, do you want me to do it or not!"

I stick out my tongue at him, which he can't see, and motion for him to continue. But it's true, we did contract him from the Cleaners Guild. It's just an unfortunate side effect that Cleaners tend to be dicks with delicate artist syndrome.

I mean who even forms a guild these days? Dicks, that's who. They banded together to protect their code, the code that gets you in, and more importantly out of a smart home undetected. So now if you want to hit a smart home, which practically all worth hitting are, you need a Cleaner. At least they guarantee success.

And Ham is a Cleaner through-and-through, exemplifies their qualities: smart, paranoid, ruthless, dickish. All qualities essential for a Cleaner.

Hopefully, I'll be rid of him soon.

"Damn," Ham says.

"Not a word a girl wants to hear—"

"The hub's on a secondary air-gap circuit. I'll have to come with you."

Coming July 2015!

www.ingramcontent.com/pod-product-compliance
Lightning Source LLC
Chambersburg PA
CBHW020650130626
46552CB00003B/1491